Harry Saves Wreck

Dr. Robert A. Ernst

Illustrated by Rose E. Grier Evans

Dr. Bob's Tales: Book 3

Discoveries Publishing, LLC
Palm Coast, Florida

Book design by Sagaponack Books & Design
Cover design by Rose E. Grier Evans

ISBNs:
978-0-9998318-8-5 (softcover)
978-0-9998318-9-2 (hardcover)
978-1-7377805-0-2 (e-book)

Library of Congress Catalog Card Number: 2021923267

Summary: Harry and his friends are dedicated to restoring the sheriff's car, Wreck, and Professor Ludwig's discovery of a rock with an electromagnetic force proves to be the answer.

JUV039060 Juvenile Fiction / Social Themes / Friendship
JUV036020 Juvenile Fiction / Technology / Inventions
JUV039220 Juvenile Fiction / Social Themes / Values & Virtues
JUV045000 Juvenile Fiction / Readers / Chapter Books

www.DrBobsTales.com

First Edition
Printed in the USA

This book is dedicated, in loving memory, to
my mother, Marie Louise Ernst,
and
my mother-in-law, Lillian Veronica Conroy.

Contents

List of Characters vi

Map of Pondville viii

Chapter 1 1

Chapter 2 11

Chapter 3 17

Chapter 4 23

Chapter 5 29

Chapter 6 35

Chapter 7 45

Chapter 8 52

Chapter 9 59

Chapter 10 64

Chapter 11 71

Chapter 12 77

Chapter 13 86

Chapter 14 94

Chapter 15 101

Chapter 16 108

About Dr. Bob's Tales 116

Discussion Guide 118

About the Pond 120

Acknowledgments. 121

About the Illustrator 122

About the Author 123

CHARACTERS IN ORDER OF APPEARANCE

Harry, a frog:
Sheriff of Pondville

Charlie, a frog:
Mechanic and builder

Wreck, a car:
Sheriff's car

Sally, a frog:
Pondville's event chairperson

Bart, a bear:
A chief deputy sheriff of Pondville

Kim, deer:
A chief deputy sheriff of Pondville

Bernie, a goose:
Pondville's doctor

Ludwig, a turtle:
Professor and inventor

Red, an ant:
General of the ant army

Stinky, a skunk:
A deputy sheriff of Pondville

Earl, a crow:
A deputy sheriff of Pondville

Percy, a turtle:
Mayor of Pondville

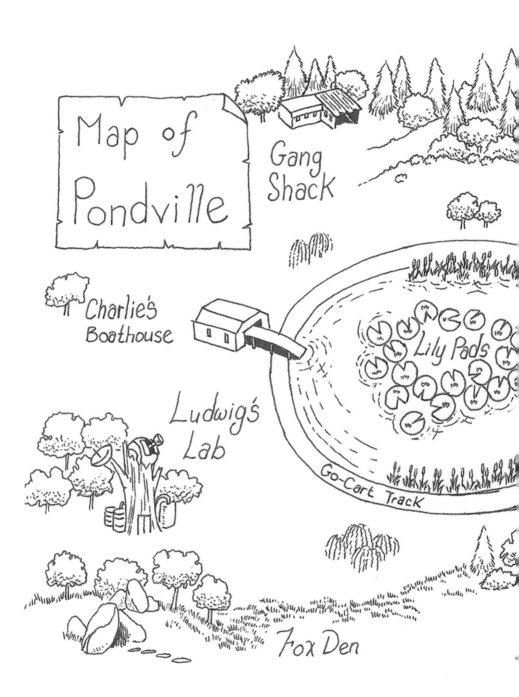

Chapter 1

It was a cool morning with a layer of fog hanging over the pond. Sheriff Harry the frog hurried on his way to Charlie's boathouse to see if the car was ready.

"Top of the morning, Charlie," said Harry.

Charlie was leaning over the car's fender, doing last-minute adjustments. The tattooed frog was wearing his baseball cap backwards. This way, the brim didn't keep banging into the car when he bent close to it.

"Morning, cuz. Just finishing up here," said Charlie, smiling as he put down a wrench. "I knew you would be by early, so I made sure your car was ready."

"How did it go with the repairs?"

Charlie shrugged and said, "I don't know. I did everything possible to keep him running. For how long? Hard to say. We'll have to keep our fingers crossed that he'll hold out."

"What did you fix?"

"Well, I changed the oil, replaced the spark plugs, and gave him a grease job. At the moment, it's all I can do."

***

"Sheriff Harry, this is headquarters. A report has just come in of a skirmish down at the tennis courts. Are you available to take the call?"

Harry looked at Charlie. "Is my car ready to roll?"

"He is all yours. By the way, this is a good opportunity to test him out."

Harry said, "Headquarters, I've got it. I'm on my way."

The frogs pushed the car out of the boathouse. Harry turned the key and the car started immediately: *Vroom, vroom.* With a shudder, the car coughed and sputtered. *Vroom, vroom,* went his car again.

Harry said, "Hmm, sounds quirky, but worth a try. Off we go!"

"Good luck," Charlie called out, waving.

***

Halfway to the tennis courts, the car bucked, slowed down, and died.

Harry threw up his arms in exasperation and yelled, "Now what?"

He picked up his radio and called headquarters. "This is Sheriff Harry. My car just conked out. No way can I make it to the disturbance. Send Chief Deputy Bart the bear and Deputy Stinky the skunk to the scene. I'll let you know if I need help here."

Harry stepped out of the car and walked around it, shaking his head in frustration.

He shook his finger at the car and said, "I don't know what I'm going to do with you. I can't junk you because there aren't enough funds to buy a new car. I am out of patience. I am stuck. Stuck with a piece of junk, a plain old wreck. Hey, that's a good name for you. *Wreck*."

Losing his cool was so out of character for Harry.

Lo and behold, the car groaned painfully, and clearly stated, "Watch it, buster. I'm sick and tired of you calling me all kinds of names and whatever. You think you're so perfect? Guess again."

Taking two quick steps backward, Harry exclaimed, "You talked to me!"

"Yeah," said the car, "and you hurt my feelings. Watch what you say about me. I am very easily offended."

Still dumbfounded, Harry repeated, "You talked to me!"

"So what? You're a talking frog. What's the difference?"

"Yeah, I know. No difference. Okay, I got it."

"You want to know why I sputtered out? I wanted to set the record straight. If and when you need me—and I know you are going to need me—I might sit there and refuse to move, just like now. You'd best apologize to me so we can clear the air."

Harry took a long pause and thought, *I can't believe what happened, but he does have a point.* Harry was upset over the fact that he was wrong and knew he must apologize.

"Hey, Sheriff, I see you're hesitating. Your apology better be from the heart, or it won't be worth a plug nickel."

Before Harry could say anything else, Sally the frog showed up. "Hi, Harry. Who are you talking to? I was out for a walk and heard you talking away. What's up?"

"Sally, have you ever heard a car talk? I was talking to my sheriff's car, and he talked right back to me."

"Oh, really? I heard he used to talk, but I wasn't around then. There were a lot of stories about him. This is super curious."

The car said, "What's your name, girlie?"

With a surprised look, Sally answered, "My name is Sally. What's yours?"

"Wreck. Your buddy, here, gave me that name."

"Pleased to meet you, Wreck."

"Likewise, Sally. Aren't you the pretty little frog who was in charge of the 15th Annual Derby Day Go-cart Race?"

"Yes. It's so nice of you to remember." Her eyelids fluttered. "So, what's going on here—or am I being too nosy?"

Harry said, "First of all, I never heard of a talking car. Second, I'm trying to get this car to run right, and it's giving me nothing but trouble. I ran out of patience with his on-again, off-again attitude when I need to go someplace. I lost it and called my car a wreck."

"Oh," Sally said, "does that hurt your feelings, Wreck?"

"Yeah, it sure does. But no one understands what I've been through. Would you like to hear some of it?"

Sally sat on a stump, smiled, and said, "Sure, if you don't get too upset."

"Yeah," Harry said, "go ahead. I'm curious."

"To start off with," Wreck stated, "I was left outside like a worthless piece of junk. That is, until Harry was appointed sheriff and the mayor gave him the keys to me."

"Oh, you poor thing," Sally said in a soft tone. "Tell me more."

"I had no one to talk to, no one to clean me when I got dirty, no one to polish my chrome. I felt sick and old and useless."

Harry was totally astounded. "I had no idea. I am so sorry."

Wreck went on. "It rained on me, it snowed on me, and pigeons pooped on me. Youngsters jumped all over me and used me to play cops and robbers. That's how my seats became lumpy. I got sicker and sicker and junkier. I looked a wreck, as someone recently said … hint, hint! I may have a few worn-out parts, but I still have my brain. I'm not a dummy, you know."

This was too much for Sally and she began to tear up. Harry's head hung down.

"I was so sad and lonely. My parents were gone, and the old sheriff left town. Nobody cared about me anymore. And I want you to know I am not as old as I look!"

After a long moment of silence, Harry said, "Sally, I was about to apologize to him when you walked up. After hearing his story, now, more than ever, I realize I was wrong. Really wrong."

Harry shuffled his feet and held out his arms in a caring gesture. He gazed directly at Wreck's headlights and said, "I am very sorry I hurt your feelings, and I promise not to do it again. This is my heartfelt apology and I don't know what more I can say. So, is that good enough?"

"Oh, let me think about it. The name is hurtful and downright gut-wrenching, right down to my inner gearbox!" Wreck paused to let Harry's apology sink in. Many thoughts swirled around: *Do I forgive or not forgive? I need to let the past go and move on with my life. I ought to give Harry a chance. Do I have any other choice? I don't think so.*

"Okay, Harry, I accept your apology. I'm a good sport. You can call me Wreck."

Sally hopped up from the stump and wiped Wreck's fender with her hankie. "Wreck," she said, "you are an inspiration to me and I'm sure you will be to others. Are you sure you can handle the name Wreck? We can always change your name to something you'll like better."

"No. The more I think about it …. It's a unique name. As a matter of fact, it's pretty unforgettable. I like it. I'll keep it."

Sally said, "Good. We've got your name settled. Believe me, Wreck, Harry's a good guy and will prove to be a true friend."

Wreck asked, "Now, what is it you want from me, Harry?"

"I want you to be part of my team and the best-running, best-looking sheriff's car ever. Wreck, let's go over to the sheriff's office to see Bart and Kim."

"Oh, I know them. They were with the last administration. They're good folks."

Harry said, "We have two new deputies, named Stinky and Earl. If they are around, I'd like to introduce you."

"I'd like that."

"Sally, want to come along?" Harry asked.

"No, thanks. I'm going to continue my walk. Time alone will give you two a chance to get to know one another better." Sally knew when to stay and when to go. "Besides, you'll be going to your office to get Wreck reacquainted with his teammates and maybe even meet the new ones."

Chapter 2

"Chief deputies, come out and see who's here." Bart the bear and Kim the deer came running out. They were flabbergasted when they saw Wreck. Neither of them knew about his situation. Since the old sheriff left town, they were so busy they hadn't given the car a thought.

Bart said, "It's been forever since I've seen you. How are you doing?"

"Now that Harry is sheriff, I think I'll be okay. I guess you didn't know or wonder about me," Wreck said, looking downward for a moment.

Kim jumped in and said, "I am so sorry. Life and work got in the way. Somehow I assumed you were okay, until I saw you after Harry's swearing-in ceremony. You deserve the best, and I will do my part to see you are well treated. I've missed our chats."

Bart stepped closer to the car. "I can only repeat what Kim said. You are so important to us and to our department. Glad to have you back. Stinky the skunk, Earl the crow, and Hapless the bloodhound aren't here right now, but you'll meet them soon. They are a great addition to our team."

Sheriff Harry stated, "Deputies, our sheriff's car has agreed to be called Wreck."

"Welcome back, Wreck." Bart greeted Wreck with open arms and a pat on his hood. "Where will you be living?"

Harry answered for him. "Wreck will be staying at Charlie's boathouse until we can get his garage cleaned out. It's full of junk and debris."

"Sheriff, let us clean it out and make it livable for Wreck. It would be our honor," Kim said. "Anyway, it's one way of making it up to Wreck for our neglect."

Bart agreed.

***

Harry and Wreck spent the next week getting to know one another while they were out on patrol. Every once in a while, Wreck would groan when Harry opened the door and got in. There were occasional episodes of backfiring or steering or stopping issues, but they didn't seem like big problems. Harry and Wreck had a great time riding around Pondville. Wreck saw folks he hadn't seen in more than a year.

The delighted residents said things such as:

"Great to see you out and about again."

"We missed you."

"Come visit and we'll talk about old times."

"Where have you been hiding?"

"You look happy."

"Harry treating you okay?"

***

Then came the day when Harry climbed into Wreck, and Wreck yelled, "Ow, ow!"

"What's wrong, Wreck?"

"Oh … nothing."

"Now, come on. I know you. Your groans tell me something's wrong. I've noticed you've been doing that more and more. I insist you tell me what's wrong."

"I haven't been feeling well lately, Sheriff. My ball joint stabilizers are aching and my energy is not so good." Wreck didn't like to admit it.

"Have you been taking your vitamins? And did you eat a good breakfast this morning?"

"Yes, I took my vitamins and I had a nice bowl of crunch-pops with iron. It always made me feel nice and strong, but it doesn't seem to be working as well as it did in the past."

"Okay. That's it. I'm going to make an appointment with Dr. Bernie the goose and have him do a check-up on you tomorrow morning."

"No, no, you don't have to do that. I'm okay."

"Oh, yes I do. Now I'm worried about you and I can't let anything happen to my best pal."

"Okay, if you insist." Wreck was beginning to feel wanted.

***

After a harrowing day, Harry went home to relax. As he sipped his orange juice, Sally the frog popped up from between the lily pads to join him.

She brushed her hair back. "Hi, Har, what's up? You have a concerned look on your face."

"Wreck told me he's not feeling well, and I'm worried about him."

"Has he had a check-up lately?"

"Not really. Charlie gave him a once-over. He is no doctor, but he did his best. When I got in to go on patrol, Wreck groaned in pain. I knew I had to take action. So I made an appointment with Doc Bernie. He'll do an evaluation on Wreck tomorrow."

"Good. I'm going with you."

With that settled, Harry and Sally spent the rest of the day swimming in the pond. The afternoon and evening flew by.

Their hearts were heavy; they worried about what Bernie's evaluation might uncover.

Chapter 3

By 9:00 a.m. the next morning, Harry and Sally were anxiously awaiting Dr. Bernie.

Bernie came well prepared, carrying his doctor's bag and with his stethoscope hanging around his neck. His bag contained all kinds of tools and wrenches—needed for a thorough exam. There were more crazy gadgets than you could imagine, and enough medical tools in Bernie's bag to evaluate Wreck from top to bottom.

Charlie the frog told Wreck, "We are going to put you on the lift so all of your car parts can be examined."

They placed him on the lift and hoisted him up.

Bernie called out, "Everybody, please leave so Wreck can have privacy during the exam."

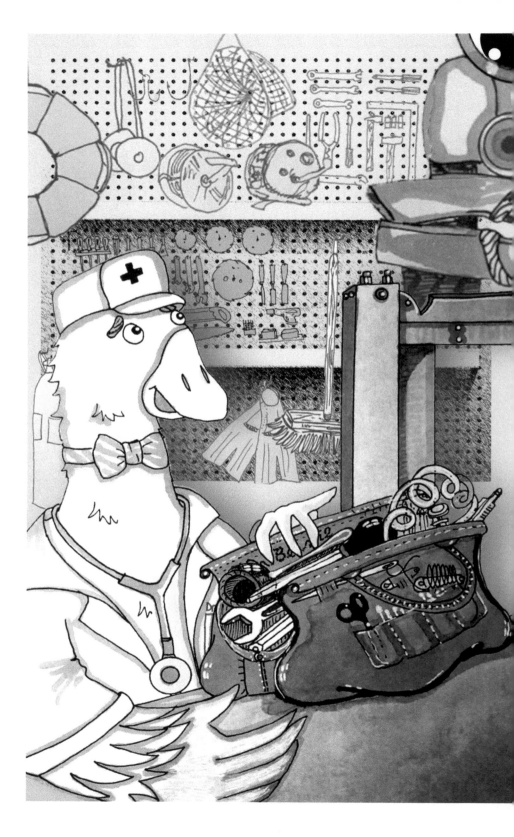

One hour passed. Harry, Sally, Charlie, and Kim paced back and forth outside the boathouse. They were concerned about what Bernie might find.

Bernie completed his check-up and had a heart-to-heart talk with Wreck.

"You're going to need surgery to replace your worn-out parts. You'll be out of commission for a day or so, and you'll need care."

"But, Doc, that means folks have to adjust their schedules to care for me. It doesn't seem fair to them."

"C'mon, get a grip. Don't you realize this is their way of showing love and respect for a neighbor? They're making a choice. If they didn't want to do this, they wouldn't. Don't you tell me that if the situation were reversed, you wouldn't do the same thing. Right or wrong?"

Wreck said, "You're right. I'm sorry."

"Eventually, you'll need an engine transplant. We'll talk about that when the time comes."

Finally, Bernie opened the doors. The goose waddled out and said, "There is good news and bad news. Come on in."

Harry said, "Doc, give us the bad news first."

"Here it is. Wreck's oil pressure is very high—so high, an oil line could burst at any time. That would not be a happy occasion! There is a high level of cholesterol in his oil and many fragments and slivers of steel floating around—they definitely contribute to his overall wear and tear. The ball joints are worn and need to be replaced. His engine is about to give out. He needs a new one."

Harry's immediate thought was: *So that's the reason he has problems climbing hills and coming to a complete stop, and for the backfiring.*

Dr. Bernie held up a tip of his wing. "Now the good news. The oil lines and ball joints can be replaced. The most difficult part is to obtain a suitable engine to replace the one he has now. We need to find the right donor and they are far and few between. I will put him on the transplant list for an engine. As soon as one is found, I'll take immediate action."

Kim said, "Can you do some repairs now, until a new engine is ready for him?"

"Yes. I recommend replacing the oil lines and ball joints right away. It will relieve any pain he is experiencing. I had a talk with Wreck about my findings. He is okay with the replacements and the possibility of a transplant."

The doctor heard big sighs of relief all around.

Bernie said, "That's not all. His biggest concern is

about putting everybody out for his caretaking. He didn't want to do that to his friends. I assured him he was well loved and he had to stop thinking that way. I told him to get a grip on himself, and it instantly put a stop to his pity party. Then Wreck said to me, 'It's better to have my problems fixed now than to be put in a junkyard to rust away!' "

The doctor crossed his arms across his chest and said, "I scheduled the first part of Wreck's surgery for tomorrow morning. Let's get him to rest up."

Harry and Sally assured Wreck they would be there for him and not to worry about anything.

Kim smiled at Wreck and said, "Don't feel guilty about putting anybody out. Everyone is eager to pitch in to help you."

"Don't worry, buddy, we've got your back," Charlie added.

Wreck was so touched, he started to shed a few tears—from the raindrops stored around his headlights. His friends escorted Wreck into the boathouse and settled him in for the night. Everyone was concerned that he get a good night's sleep.

"Thanks, everybody," Wreck said. He closed his headlights and felt a rush of joy to have such caring friends.

The lights went out and the doors closed.

Chapter 4

The next morning, Bernie strolled down the hill with a crew of interns and nurses, each pulling a wagon of auto parts.

Pondville was a small town, and news had traveled fast about Wreck's surgery.

Charlie opened the doors to the boathouse and brought Wreck to the door. A crowd had gathered to wish Wreck a successful operation.

What joy he felt—all these folks cared that much for him!

As Wreck waved goodbye to his supporters, they broke out in loud cheering and a long round of applause.

The doors closed.

Harry and Charlie gently placed him on the lift for the operation. Wreck gave a groan as he settled into a comfortable position. The surgical attendees put on their gloves and face masks.

Harry and Charlie exited the boathouse to wait until Bernie and his crew had completed the surgery.

***

In his soft bedside voice, Bernie said, "Wreck, the first thing I'll do to prepare you for surgery is give you anesthesia, so you won't feel any pain."

You could feel Bernie's confidence as he prepared for the operation.

"Okay, Doc, I'm ready."

Sedating Wreck was not a simple procedure. Bernie grunted when he hopped up on the lift. He opened a special adapter with plastic tubes attached to the areas that needed numbing.

"Nurse, turkey baster, please."

Bernie filled the turkey baster with a local anesthetic and squirted the liquid into the adapter. He squeezed the little bulb several times to empty the contents into the adapter.

"Nurse, toilet plunger, please."

He placed the plunger over the adapter and started to pump it up and down. The plunger forced anesthesia through the tubes. Bernie exerted a lot of energy doing this procedure. When he pushed down and came back up to release the pressure, it was like being on a seesaw. His white goose head and wings went down and his back end came up and then his head and wings went up and his back end went down. In a flurry, he kept it up until the anesthesia got to all the right places. A few feathers even flew off the doctor's body and landed at his feet.

"Nurse, wipe, please." Sweat was building on his brow.

The problem for Bernie was that sometimes his tail feathers got tangled up in a wad. When he was finished with the procedure, he jumped off the lift and gave his back end a good swirl to untangle the feathers. Unfortunately, he lost a few more feathers and some of them ended up flying around.

The anesthesia nurse checked the patient's progress and reported that Wreck's oil pressure was 120/80, his breathing was good, and he was out. The operation was under way.

Many hours passed.

Harry, Sally, Charlie, and many others were sitting and standing outside, waiting patiently.

Still, everybody felt tense. They hoped nothing would go wrong.

How much longer?

The boathouse doors opened and out came the surgical crew—some helping Wreck along to a cluster of microphones.

Bernie spoke first. "I want everybody to know that the operation was a complete success. From the standpoint of the replacement parts, Wreck is as good as new."

Everybody clapped and cheered at Bernie's announcement.

Then Wreck rolled up to the microphones. "I want to thank all of you for your support. I want to thank the doctors and nurses for their valiant efforts to make me well enough so I can get around more comfortably. I will be forever in their debt. Thank you, thank you."

Everybody cheered and clapped again.

Harry walked up to Wreck. "We are here for you. Let's get you settled comfortably in the boathouse so you can rest and recover."

Wreck indeed rested comfortably and enjoyed lots of TLC—tender loving care.

***

Kim and Bart cleared out the garage and it was all set for the sheriff's car. They moved Wreck into his home two days after his surgery. Every day, he had visitors stopping by to say hi and to check on him. The TLC continued!

Chapter 5

Professor Ludwig the turtle, a true rocket scientist, stepped outside his lab. It was a bright sparkling day, not a cloud in the sky, and the temperature was cool. A slight breeze was blowing. It felt good when it fanned his face. *What a great day for exploring!*

He grabbed his backpack and took a hike up and over the hill. His mission today was to find stinkweed and, if lucky, find some geological specimens. Last year a virus attacked Pondville's turtles and almost wiped them out. Ludwig knew some of them had eaten stinkweed and were cured. Naturally, he thought there was a connection between the deadly virus and stinkweed. His plan was to find the weed, bring some back to the lab, and develop a serum for a vaccination.

As the professor headed up the second hill, he started to huff and puff. *Boy, I'm not as young as I used to be. ... This hill gets steeper and steeper as time goes by. ... Finally, I'm at the top. ... I think I'll stand here and catch my breath and take in the scenery.*

Let me see. Hmm. I see some patches of weeds on the other side of this field. I'll cut across the field to take a look.

As he got nearer, he said, "What's that I smell? Let me get a closer look."

Sure enough, it was a small patch of stinkweed, all flattened out. "Must have been some deer camping out. I can see a small stone fireplace with ashes."

While inspecting the weed, he decided to scratch around and search for seedpods. It would be most convenient if he could grow stinkweed in his lab.

The brainy turtle reached in his backpack and pulled out a three-pronged claw to scratch away some dirt. After a minute or so, he uncovered something strange, and he scraped the dirt aside.

"What's this?" He peered through his magnifying glass. ... It was glowing. The black dirt was crusty and caked on. He kept talking aloud to himself—normal for Ludwig. "I want to get this back to my lab and see what it is. Let me clean off a small area. I need a better look at it."

He took out his excavating brush and cleaned the strange object. It was hard and it gave off an eerie light that produced vivid colors, like a rainbow on steroids. Scratching his head, Ludwig thought, *This is extraordinary. What could it be? What could it be?*

He reached down and pulled a large piece of rock out of the ground. "Hmm, very interesting." Ludwig opened his backpack and placed his new find near his other specimens. All of a sudden, other rocks he had picked up along the way moved over a few inches.

Ludwig's eyes opened wide. His excitement and curiosity soared. He exclaimed, "Wow, look at that! I can't believe what I just saw."

All kinds of thoughts started going through his head. *Is this a brand-new discovery? How the heck did it get here? How long has it been buried here?*

Smart guy that he was, Ludwig knew he must do two things: keep the spot secret and be able to find his way back here.

He paced back and forth. "What to do next? I'll draw a map, of course." He took out his notebook and pen to draw the map.

The moment after he bent his head down to concentrate on drawing, he heard some twigs snapping.

He looked up and saw Bertha the bear come running, in a big hurry.

As she flew by him, Bertha's heart was racing. "Hey, Professor, you'd better vamoose out of here. I was attacked by swarms of fire ants. They were biting and stinging me everywhere. The only way I could get them off was to run as fast as I could and keep slapping at them. I'm outta here. Never coming here again. See ya."

Ludwig waved to Bertha, relieved that she was hightailing it out of the area.

Whew, that was a close one!

He began to draw the treasure map. The first thing was to put an *X* on the map to mark the spot. Then he drew different landmarks—the large elm tree, the babbling brook, and two big boulders. Next he paced them out from *X* and wrote the distances on the map.

Ludwig never went exploring without a compass. He used it to determine the direction from *X* to his lab and wrote that down. All he had to do to return to the spot was reverse the direction.

He covered up the area with leaves and twigs to make it appear natural and untouched.

Great job. Nobody can tell the area was disturbed. What a genius I am!

He decided to name his find "X-rock."

Chapter 6

Ludwig strapped on his backpack and headed to the lab. Hiking across the field Bertha had come from, he approached a huge group of pine and oak trees. Many had fallen down due to storms and were rotting away.

Lo and behold, he came across a little mound of dirt under a rotted tree. Startled, he noticed thousands of red ants scurrying around in a panic. On top of the log, a larger than normal ant, holding a bullhorn, was yelling out orders.

Spotting Ludwig, he said, "Hey, turtle, if I were you, I'd get my shell out of here as fast as I could. If you don't, you'll be sorry. We don't need any foreigners poking around our colony."

"No problem," said Ludwig. "I noticed there seemed to be trouble here. I wondered if I could help out in some way. If not, I'm on my way out of here."

"Hold on, then. That's very kind of you to offer to help. By the way, my name is Red. Maybe there is a way you could help us out. I'm the head honcho here."

Red stepped off the log, put his bullhorn down, and shook Ludwig's hand.

"We do have a problem," Red explained, and several of his six legs gestured to act out his words. "The rotted log shifted, trapped our queen, and she can't move or get out.

Rocks are surrounding her and the log is on top of her. We're trying to move the log enough for her to escape."

"If you will allow me, I'd be happy to help."

Red knew he needed help. His army couldn't do the job fast enough to save her. They were running out of time. If they didn't get the log off quickly, they'd lose their queen. That would be the end of the colony.

Red said to Ludwig, "Okay, you get in the middle of the log and push it while my men push from the other end. By the way, what's your name?"

"I go by Professor Ludwig."

Red picked up the bullhorn and said clearly, "Everybody, listen up. This turtle, here, has volunteered to help us out. I want you to treat him with respect. Don't any of you get any ideas that he is our enemy and attack him. You'll feel my wrath if you do. And you know that won't be pleasant! On the count of three, push. ... Ready? ... One, two, three, push. ... Push."

The log moved ever so slightly. Was it enough for the queen to break free?

It was a long, tense moment.

Silence.

Oh, the waiting!

This meant so much to the colony.

It was a matter of life or death.

A few more seconds later, the queen poked her head out and then scampered into the fresh air.

Loud cheering erupted from the colony.

Ludwig was deeply touched by the emotion and loyalty shown by her subjects. A slight tear appeared at the corner of his eye.

Red helped the queen up to a mound of sand. "Your Majesty, this is Professor Ludwig. With his help, we were able to save you."

Ludwig bowed respectfully to the queen. He stood there proudly, alongside the army of ants.

"I offer my sincere gratitude to you, Professor. We will forever be deeply indebted to you. I was terrified in that deep, dark dungeon. My wings were caught and I couldn't move at all." The queen was still shaking from her ordeal.

The queen turned to Red and said, "I want to make Professor Ludwig an honorary member of our colony, with all the rights and privileges granted to him.

"Red, please hand me my sword and an official sash."

The purple sash was *V* shaped. Along its edges, inside and outside, was a yellow stripe and gold fringe.

"Professor, please kneel." The queen placed the sword on one of the turtle's shoulders, and then the other, and stated, "I dub thee Sir Ludwig, an honorary knight of my colony." She placed the sash over him.

Bowing, Ludwig said, in a strong voice, "Thank you, Your Majesty. I am deeply honored."

"Red, make sure he is issued a permanent passport to our colony."

After the ceremony, Red said to Ludwig, "Wait here for me. Right now, I need to escort our queen to her secure domain."

Red turned and spoke to the army. "Everybody, back to work. No slacking. We've got to get everything shipshape. That means giving it your all."

Ludwig stood there thinking, *What an honor! I wonder if it means I don't have to worry about being attacked when I come through here. Maybe I can get them to set up some outposts around the perimeter where I found the X-rock. That would be so great. They could protect the discovery area, and I wouldn't have to worry about anybody else coming across it.*

About ten minutes later, Red came back and approached Ludwig. "As the queen stated, we are indebted to you. You are now an honorary knight of our colony. Here is your passport. We are at your beck and call. Is there anything that you immediately wish for us to do?"

"Not really. When I realized you were in dire straits, my only concern was for the safety of the colony."

Ludwig figured he should not be pushy or demanding in any way, thinking, *Let me wait it out and see how it goes.*

Red said, "I noticed you were digging over there. Anything special you were looking for?"

"Yes. I was searching for stinkweed. I need it to make a serum to vaccinate Pondville's turtles. Last year a virus hit our turtle population, and the thing that destroyed the virus was stinkweed. I want to develop a serum that will protect us in the future." He was careful not to give away his discovery of X-rock.

"Good to know. From what I have seen, you have abilities that could benefit all types of life. It's great that you're on our team now. Who knows where this could lead?"

Ludwig sensed this was the right time. "Red, there is a favor I might ask of you. Would you be willing to set up some outposts around the area? I'd like to keep it private so no one will destroy my growing and digging area."

"Consider it done. Always glad to be of service. As soon as we clean up this mess, that will be the first item on my to-do list."

"Thank you, Red. Now I think I'll return to my lab and continue with my work."

Red waved and said, "Thanks again. Keep in touch."

***

As Ludwig hiked down the hill closest to his lab, his head swirled with excitement, thinking about the day's discoveries. In general, turtles were slow moving, but not today. Ludwig's only problem in going fast—*fast* in Ludwig's mind—was keeping his balance. He tripped over small pebbles and rocks along his path. It was like a bumpy ride. *Boy, am I ever glad I have such good balance!*

During his bouncy journey, it seemed the specimens in his backpack were moving around erratically. *Did something sneak into my backpack?*

He stopped and stared inside to see what the problem was. The X-rock was isolated. *Hmm. No sign of any critters. The other objects have moved away from it. Or maybe the others pushed X-rock away!*

In all his studies, Ludwig had never once come across anything like this. He couldn't get back to the lab fast enough. He tightened the backpack straps, not wanting to chance losing any specimens.

***

The professor stepped into his lab and pulled every geology book out of his bookcase. He wanted to see what he could learn about X-rock or any rock even slightly similar.

Ludwig performed every test imaginable on X-rock. After four days he concluded that he had discovered a mysterious electromagnetic force. X-rock moved objects. He hopped for a few seconds and danced around the lab, bouncing from foot to foot.

The test results amazed him. He could control the speed of movement of any object by rubbing X-rock. The more he tested, the more possibilities showed up. It was possible to steer with X-rock—making it move objects in any direction—based on the area rubbed. Overall findings: Rubbing causes friction, increasing heat, and causing an increase in electromagnetic force (EMF). The force controls the speed and direction of an object.

Light bulbs (and there were many) went off in Ludwig's head. *Of course the objects moved away from X-rock when I was walking. All the bouncing rubbed X-rock. That's it! What a phenomenon!*

Endless possibilities could result from his discovery, both good and bad. But something kept cautioning him: *Keep it a secret! Who knows what could happen if X-rock gets into the wrong hands!*

Chapter 7

Ludwig's brilliant mind was spinning. Ideas kept popping into his head. They traveled the pathways of his brain—like a journey through jumbled wires. The ideas went every which way, yet were somehow organized. Go figure! The harder and harder he thought, the faster and faster he jotted down his concepts.

"What can I invent that will benefit all who live in Pondville?"

This solitary thinking was great. That was the way Ludwig came up with many of his outstanding inventions. But this major discovery called for sharing ideas with a friend and fellow inventor. Together, they would come up with even better uses. Charlie came to mind as the person to team up with. Charlie could be trusted. And he was a first-class builder! Before calling on Charlie, Ludwig organized his ideas into different categories. After all, he was the kind of turtle that wanted to take charge of a brainstorming session.

One idea was to build a rocket propelled by X-rock. *How often might anyone in Pondville need a rocket?* Even better was a rocket and car, all in one—a rocket-mobile. That would be a lot more practical. Maybe it would be as simple as adding wheels to switch from a rocket to a car. True to form, he got carried away and still hadn't talked to Charlie. Ludwig could be absentminded!

Ludwig envisioned how a rocket-mobile should look: It would have a bullet-shaped hood, like a racing car, and wings with movable flaps that create stability. There was always the problem of rocking up and down. A tail with two smaller wings with movable flaps would prevent this. To stop side swinging, there would be a fin—similar to a shark's—which stuck straight up out of the tail. After all, no passenger wants to be swaying from side to side when they're flying. So Ludwig had a design already worked out in his head.

Of course, figuring out how the rock would be rubbed and placed was a whole other problem to be tackled. On to the next step!

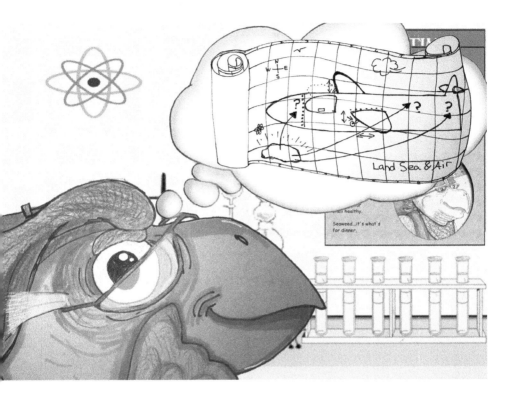

Off he went to visit Charlie … finally.

Ludwig found Charlie sitting on his dock, dangling his feet in the water and catching rays. He wore the usual Hawaiian shirt and a baseball cap to keep the sun out of his eyes. His rocket-shaped boat was tied alongside.

"What's up, Professor? Anything exciting?"

"Charlie, I have something amazing to discuss with you. Let's go to my lab. It's very hush-hush."

"Sure thing, Ludwig."

***

Ludwig said, "I want your support with my latest and greatest project. If you accept, you must swear to keep the plan top secret."

"You can rely on me to keep it secret. My lips are sealed." Charlie ran his fingers over his mouth like closing a zipper.

Ludwig responded with a nod of his head and a slight smile. "My project involves the construction of a rocket-mobile," he said in a serious voice. "With your help, we can make this work. Let me explain some of the details. Remember, everything I tell you must be kept secret." Ludwig told Charlie about finding a weird rock, and how it could propel objects. "Who knows where we can go with this?"

"Yeah. Don't stop," said the frog. He perched at the edge of his seat.

"You and I must be the only ones who know about the existence of X-rock. If it got into the wrong hands, it could put our community in grave danger. Besides, we may develop something super-duper, and who knows where it will take us! Let me give you some examples I've been thinking about. We could convert a car to go as fast as lightning. Maybe get it to fly. Build a rocket. Make a super ray gun. Someone could put a backpack on and fly."

"Fantastic, unbelievable! Count me in." Charlie jumped off the stool and gave Ludwig a fist bump.

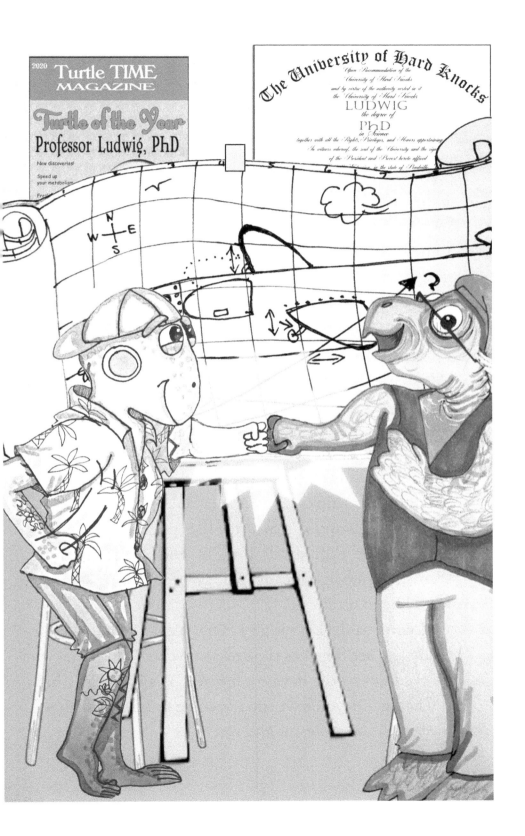

"This gets my juices flowing. Oh, please count me in."

Charlie moved backward a couple of inches and said, "Ludwig, before we go any further, why don't we bring in Sheriff Harry? After all, he won the go-cart derby the past four years. He always manages to come up with something and, even better, he outsmarts anyone who comes up against him ... like both of us."

"You're right. Three heads would be better than two. Harry is a whiz when it comes to speed." Ludwig, however, did not like the reference to losing the derby; the memory distracted him.

"After all," Charlie said, still trying to convince his friend, "he is the sheriff, and we both know how trustworthy he is. He can provide protection and also keep snoops away while we're building and testing. What do you think?"

Ludwig snapped back to the present. "I agree, Charlie. We should fill him in and swear him to secrecy." Ludwig already felt safer, knowing Harry would be in on it.

Charlie said, "Let me give Harry a call on the walkie-talkie and see if he has time to come over."

He went to the device a few feet away. "Harry, this is Charlie. Do you have time to come to Ludwig's lab to meet with the professor and me?"

Harry's radio had a bit of static. "Charlie, I'm tied up right now, but I can be over in an hour."

"See you then. Over and out."

Excited by the possibilities, Charlie and Ludwig kept talking, often interrupting one another.

Chapter 8

Harry popped through the lab's doorway an hour and a half later. Charlie and Ludwig were still in deep discourse, oblivious to the world around them.

"Hi, guys. Sorry I'm late, but it took longer than expected."

"No problem, cuz," Charlie said. "Have a seat over here. I'm turning this meeting over to Ludwig. He'll bring you up-to-date."

As calmly as he could, Ludwig said, "Harry, hold on to your sheriff's hat. What I am about to tell you is mind-blowing."

The professor talked in detail about everything he had already told Charlie. Every once in a while, Charlie added something that Ludwig forgot to mention. Ludwig had a tendency to forget. Harry sat there, listening intently.

After a lengthy and complex explanation, Ludwig let out a deep sigh and asked, "What do you think, Harry?"

"Whew, wow, unbelievable." For once, Harry was speechless. He got up and walked around, releasing some pent-up energy. Finally, he blurted out, "You're right, this is mind-blowing! The possibilities are endless. You mentioned that this must be kept secret."

"Yes, I believe so," said Ludwig.

Instantly, Harry said, "Are you kidding me! Secrecy is of the utmost importance. Anyone who is brought into our confidence must swear to tell no one. And I mean, *no one*."

"Couldn't agree more, cuz," Charlie said.

"Let's face it," Harry said, "we each bring unique and special talent to the table. What a great team we make. Let's get on it right now. Professor, please take the lead."

"Thank you, Harry. We'll put our heads together and figure out where we can go with this."

"Before we do anything," Harry said, "let's make sure the doors are closed tightly and locked."

Charlie took care of the doors.

"I'll pull up the whiteboard, and we'll get to work." Ludwig grabbed a marker, clearly in charge. "My big idea is to create a rocket-mobile which can convert from a rocket to a car and vice versa." Ludwig was bursting with pride. "How does that idea hit you?"

"Gutsy and brilliant," said Charlie. "How about designing it like one of our go-carts or my boat?"

"You know," replied Ludwig, "that thought already crossed my mind."

Charlie always had great ideas—for example, his creative tattoos!

They came up with a blueprint for a rocket-mobile. It had all the bells and whistles that Ludwig wanted and a few new ones that Charlie contributed. They both had big grins on their faces.

Harry had been quiet as he focused on a good project to start with. "Let me give my two cents' worth. Your idea is groundbreaking and something we should pursue ... later, not now."

Ludwig was taken aback. "What? What do you mean?"

"Here's what I propose. Let's start simple and concentrate on a car first. Once we have that working, we can go on to a rocket or anything else."

Charlie chimed in. "Makes sense. Why don't we go to the auto recycling yard and pick out the most promising car."

Harry couldn't hold back. "Wait a minute. What about Wreck? He's very sick and getting sicker every day because he needs an engine transplant. Doc Bernie has no idea when or if we'll find a new engine in time to save Wreck's life. I am beside myself with worry. It could give Wreck a new start on life."

Ludwig asked, "Is it that serious?"

"Yes," Charlie and Harry said at the same time.

"I forgot about Wreck. He would make a perfect candidate."

Charlie said, "I did some work on Wreck and it didn't even come close to giving him a normal life. Luckily, Doc Bernie came into the picture and fixed him up pretty good, but not enough to completely restore him. He still needs a new engine."

"Okay. Let's do the car first," said Ludwig. The more he thought about it, the more he warmed to the idea. "We could help Wreck, and learn a lot about how the rock would work in the real world. We can concentrate on replacing the power component of a regular engine. Back to the drawing board, boys."

Now came the hard part: how do you drive and rub the rock? All this was happening because Ludwig found a weird rock!

Ludwig said, "Let's break for now so we can roll things around in our heads. We should plan to meet tomorrow at 1:00 p.m."

Charlie and Harry agreed. Sometimes they had to let go and give an idea some breathing room, and come back fresh. With Ludwig in charge, the discussions wore them out. What a guy!

Harry couldn't wait to tell Wreck something to give him hope. Tomorrow morning would be the perfect time, when he and Sally took him out for his exercise.

Chapter 9

The sprinkle had turned into a light rain. Harry and Sally were strolling around the pond, under an umbrella.

"Sally, let's get Wreck out for a roll. His tires need to turn and his joints need exercise."

"Good idea."

Since Wreck had no top, they set up a large umbrella which covered all the open space inside the car. It worked out great, and the rain rolled right off the umbrella. The best thing about the rain was that it gave Wreck a bath, rinsing off the dirt which had built up.

Harry and Sally strolled beside Wreck as he rolled along, just barely. You could tell he still wasn't feeling well—he backfired every once in a while, making Harry and Sally jump each time.

After one of the backfires—a heart-stopping one—Wreck blurted out, "Sorry! Can't help it."

They understood.

Sally went over to the edge of the pond to observe some water bugs swimming around. She hoped to catch one for a quick snack.

Harry and Wreck kept moving. Harry could see Wreck was going downhill fast, metaphorically, and decided to tell him that hope was on the way.

"Listen, Wreck—this is top secret. Ludwig has been working on a way to give you a transplant that will make you run like your old self, and maybe even better. You know Ludwig. If anyone can do it, he can."

Wreck scrunched his grille into a frown. "Harry, how can we be sure it will work?"

"Listen carefully! Ludwig, Charlie, and I formed a team to develop a way to replace your engine. We will take every precaution. It's experimental, but I trust Ludwig and Charlie, and I know you trust me. None of us want to see you hurt in any way. We're already working on the design and will move forward quickly."

"I'm in, Harry."

Harry opened his right hand. Wreck lifted his left front tire and they slapped them together in excitement for a high five.

Sally caught up with them and asked, "What's going on?"

At the same time, Harry and Wreck answered, "Just guy stuff."

***

They continued to stroll and roll, and then brought Wreck home. He was exhausted. His repaired parts were working fine, but it was easy to see his engine problem was getting worse.

"Wreck, will you be able to go on patrol with me tomorrow?" Harry asked, already knowing the answer. Wreck needed the exercise and the feeling of being useful.

"You bet. Nothing cranks up my gears like going on patrol and talking to folks." The big grin on Wreck's grille said it all.

***

"Harry, what's going on? You're not usually so secretive." One thing Sally disliked was being left out of the loop.

Harry knew he had to tell Sally something about it, or she wouldn't stop bugging him.

"Good news, Sally. Ludwig is working on a solution to Wreck's engine dilemma."

A huge smile spread across Sally's face. She hummed her favorite tune as she headed to the pond.

Chapter 10

That afternoon, the boathouse was steaming from the massive brainpower at work.

The turtle and the two frogs discussed four or five ideas and discarded them. It was frustrating. It took time to develop an idea and see if it could work, but time wasn't on their side. Despite all that brainpower, they were not able to connect a relationship between a working engine and the moving parts of the car. What was the missing link?

Ludwig punched himself on the forehead, jumped up, and said, "Wait a minute, something just hit me hard. Are the doors locked and windows shut?"

"Yup, don't worry. It's the first thing I do before we start our meetings," Charlie answered.

"This is it! You are going to love my idea," Ludwig said, with his chest puffed out.

"I'm all ears," said Charlie.

Harry said, "I'm with you."

"Here's the thing," Ludwig said. "The other ideas didn't work out because we didn't use the car's mechanisms as part of the solution. Right? This is what we need to do. The car's steering wheel, ignition, gas pedal, brake, and gearshift should work with a gizmo, not separate from it."

"Okay, that makes sense. Tell us more," Charlie said, sitting on the edge of his seat.

Harry sat there, rubbing his chin.

"The gizmo will have four arms with rollers, to rub X-rock. One arm is for forward, one for reverse, one for right turn, and another for left turn. Can you build the gizmo, Charlie?"

Charlie tilted his head back and grinned. "Piece of cake, as long as I have a design."

"The details," Ludwig said. "First of all, the gizmo will be powered by a unique battery—one that I'll design and build. When the driver starts the car with the usual key, it will activate the battery and the gizmo

will be in play." Ludwig tried not to get caught up in lengthy technical explanations, but it was hard for him to keep it simple.

"Ludwig, I'm with you, so far," Charlie said. "The battery is attached to the gizmo ... right?"

"Yes, exactly. We'll need a new dial on the dashboard to show the battery supply. When it is down to 15 percent power, a red light will shine to indicate it needs recharging. Can you build such a dial and attach it to the battery?"

"Another piece of cake."

"This is how I see it working. The car's mechanisms tell the gizmo what to do. The key activates the gizmo's battery. The gas pedal makes it go fast or slow by controlling the amount of rubbing. The brake slows down or stops the car completely by controlling the amount of rubbing. The steering wheel tells the gizmo what direction to go in, and the arms move accordingly. The gearshift tells the gizmo whether to go forward or in reverse."

Ludwig's face was flushed. He felt exhilarated, exhausted, and thirsty all at the same time. He reached in his knapsack, took out a canteen, and drank some water.

Charlie said, "I see what you mean by the car's devices working with the gizmo. So, if I've got it right, you want me to build the gizmo and attach it to the mechanisms. You also want me to build the dial and attach it to the battery." Charlie was in his glory, knowing what he'd build and how the parts would work together.

"Yes, you've got it. Overall, what do you think?" Ludwig glanced at the face of one friend and then the other.

"I'd say you have done it," Charlie said. "This idea will work. Let's put a plan in place to get it started." He clapped his hands once, eager to begin.

Harry had been quiet while the ideas floated around, and now he said, "I have a few concerns. What happens when the battery dies?"

Ludwig said, "It would be an eight-hour battery that's rechargeable."

"Great. What about a backup?"

"Good idea. We can store a backup in Wreck's trunk. I'm thinking about two charging stations: one in his garage and one at my lab."

"My next concern," the sheriff said, "is that without a transplant, Wreck's days are numbered. We don't have time to build a prototype."

Charlie said, "But we'd be experimenting on Wreck."

Harry crossed his arms and lowered his voice. "Without divulging any secrets, I told Wreck we were working on finding a solution, and he accepted the risk of doing something experimental."

Ludwig said, "Good. Charlie, get me the dimensions for the engine. I'll cut the X-rock to make a piece that fits. When we're finished here, I'll head over to my lab to cut and shape a section of X-rock. I'll store the X-rock for the transplant in a locked cabinet, along with the extra pieces."

His eyes glowed with excitement. "Okay, teammates, let's move forward. Back to the whiteboard."

They worked on a plan to get the gizmo built and tested. As usual, Ludwig's mind went to the technology. Charlie's went to what he had to build to make it work. Harry's went to visualizing how he would drive with the gizmo.

***

They invited Doc Bernie to the boathouse to bring him into the inner circle.

Harry started off by emphasizing the need for secrecy and that only four would be in the know.

"Doc, Ludwig has made a discovery. We believe it is the answer to Wreck's need for a transplant. I'll let Ludwig explain it to you. Charlie and I will fill in the blanks, as needed."

"My curiosity is certainly aroused," said Bernie.

Ludwig took the lead and showed Bernie the drawings. Since Bernie had operated on Wreck, he understood how all the parts would work.

"Bernie, you should be involved from now on, to help troubleshoot any problems we uncover," Ludwig said. "You may see easier ways to do this and you can identify any pitfalls. Welcome to the team."

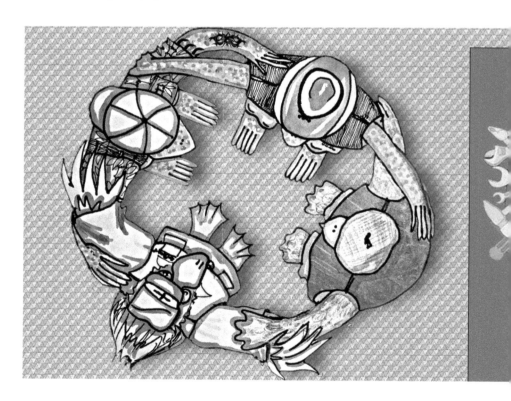

Chapter 11

The gizmo was ready in three days. Testing went well and the team was ecstatic.

Ludwig outlined the plans for Wreck's transplant the next morning.

"Harry, make the arrangements with Bernie and his team, and with Wreck, to ensure he is ready and here on time."

Turning to Charlie, the professor said, "Please prepare the boathouse for Wreck. As soon as you are done, head on over to my lab to pick up the X-rock piece, the gizmo, and the battery component. The X-rock is in the locked cabinet. I've written down the combination for you. Don't forget to cover the rock with a blanket. Meanwhile, I'll go over the final details to make sure I didn't miss anything."

Dr. Bernie put his two cents in. "By the way, Harry, make sure Wreck has a thorough bath. This should include his dashboard, grille, and wheel hubs, where dirt is easily collected. Most of all, make sure he doesn't smell or have bad breath. I need to keep my head clear at all times. It's easy to make mistakes with a foggy brain. I don't function well under stinky conditions."

"Got it. The last thing we need, Doc, is you fainting from bad breath and body odor!"

***

At 7:30 a.m. the next day, down the hill waddled Bernie the goose, along with his surgical team. He carried his stethoscope and his doc bag and some spare parts—not too many since they didn't anticipate any problems. Besides, if an emergency occurred, the supply depot was around the corner. No problem there.

When Bernie had told the team about the transplant, he did not let them in on the X-rock factor.

***

Wreck was awake most of the night—nervous about the upcoming procedure. He was ready when Harry and Sally came by to pick him up.

Harry said, "Did you shower and clean yourself inside and out?"

"Sure did." He answered the way a child would, when a parent asked: "Did you clean your room?" Why, of course the response was "Sure did."

At this time, Bernie and his crew, Charlie, and Ludwig were in front of the boathouse, waiting for Wreck. Harry and Sally strode beside Wreck as he slowly rolled along. Everybody was wide-awake, chatting away, and ready to go. Wreck gave out a big yawn; after all, he had not slept very well.

Word of a second surgery spread, and Pondville residents showed up to support Wreck again.

Some carried banners that read: GOOD LUCK, WRECK.

He was deeply touched by the love and support from the community.

***

They rolled Wreck into the boathouse and gave him a pre-surgery inspection.

"Did you shower and clean yourself off?" Ludwig asked Wreck.

"Sure did."

"Bernie and I are going to check you out to see if your cleaning is acceptable."

Wreck thought, *Oh-oh, I hope I'm not in trouble!*

"All right. Lift up your right tire and let me look underneath. ...... Dirt! It's way up high and out of sight, under the wheel hub." Ludwig frowned in disgust.

"Sorry!"

Ludwig barked out orders. "Get the cleaning team in here to hose and scrub that out."

Luckily, the other three tire areas were clean.

After the hosing, Ludwig reported, "He passed inspection. Let's roll him into the operating area."

***

Bernie put on a surgical cap and slipped a mask over his beak. His beak was long and had a funny flat area. So his mask was extra-long and shaped differently.

"Ludwig, Charlie, put on your masks and caps. Be ready when I need you."

Bernie advised Harry and Sally to try and keep busy to occupy their minds while the surgical crew did their thing. It required a lot of meticulous work and they didn't want to be pressured into hurrying.

"The surgery could take most of the day," the doctor said.

Harry and Sally went outside.

Chapter 12

Wreck was placed on the lift while the surgical team huddled around, leaning over, and inspecting the engine compartment. Bernie started preparations for the anesthesia.

He placed a wide cup over Wreck's grille and told him, "Take some deep breaths. You might feel some light-headedness. It's normal, because I am giving you laughing gas. You may experience some weird dreams, but not to worry."

Bernie smiled inwardly, thinking of all the dreams—from eerie to downright hilarious—his patients had recounted to him in the past.

As Bernie administered the gas, Wreck laughed a little. Then the laughing got more frequent and louder, and louder. Finally, Bernie quieted him down by talking to him in a soft, soothing voice. Wreck went into a deep sleep.

***

Wreck started dreaming that he had met his dream car. There she was—a white convertible with gorgeous headlights, a wax job to die for, and bright, shiny chrome sparkling in all the right places.

To top it off, she winked at Wreck as if to say, "Hey, handsome, I dig your style." It was instant love for both! He dreamt he was in a carefree world and they loved life to the fullest. They would hold tires together and roll along. It was a fantasy so indescribable, he wanted it to go on forever.

As the dream progressed, he imagined they had twin baby Wrecks and were enjoying a picnic out in the field, with a beautiful blue sky and fluffy white clouds passing by. The young Wrecks were rolling up and down the hill—whizzing around, kicking up dust and dirt, and getting filthy, like any other young cars playing around. Then he saw them roasting marshmallows—toasty and crispy—around a fire pit. Wreck pictured a marshmallow in his grille, and the love of his life pulling her grille next to his and eating the same marshmallow with him.

Meanwhile, Bernie and Ludwig connected and disconnected the various lines that made Wreck a complete car—all this was done with gentleness, to ensure his comfort. Without warning, one of the oil lines burst and squirted them in the face—the line was moving and flying around, out of control.

Nurse Louise noticed the pressure gauge was falling rapidly—normal was 120/80—and the current reading was 80/60. She alerted the team. "We are losing him. We need to clamp off the line and suture it back in."

"I need a C-clamp," yelled Bernie.

The line was still flying around uncontrollably when Nurse Abby, the trauma nurse, tackled the line and held on to it for dear life.

At that moment, Wreck flatlined—no pulse, no heartbeat, no anything. Wreck was still under anesthesia. He saw flashes similar to lightning bolts and heard loud booms resembling thunder. Then all was quiet … and he felt incredible peace and serenity—such vivid beauty and harmony! As he moved along a meadow, he enjoyed the sweet fragrance of flowers and the soft sound of peaceful music.

"Don't go. Come back to Pondville."

Wreck wasn't sure if he dreamt the words or if someone actually called to him. He felt the tug of both worlds.

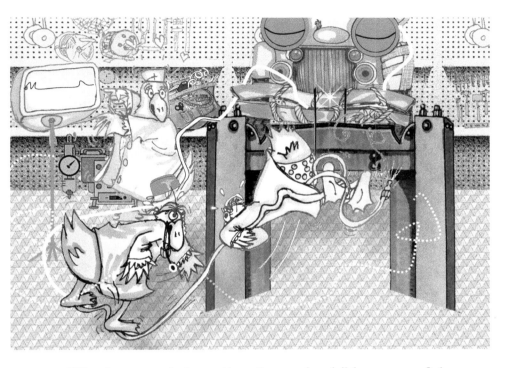

Wreck resisted the call to "come back" because of the wonderful feeling. He was at peace—which he didn't want to lose.

He knew he should go back for the sake of all those who loved, needed, and adored him. It was the more powerful call. He knew he had to decide. Wreck ended his beautiful and peaceful journey.

The moment Wreck had flatlined, the surgical team had gone into action. Bernie quickly used his big webbed right foot to step on the line and hold it still. Nurse Abby was still sitting on the line when Ludwig applied the

C-clamp to shut off the spurting oil. Next, Bernie was able to smooth both ends off and suture them together.

One of the other trauma nurses announced, "He is coming back. Pressure 90/65, 110/70, 120/80 ... he's back!"

They completed most of the mechanical connections, and were ready to install a platform to Wreck's mainframe, to be held in place with nuts and bolts. The engine was completely removed and replaced with the platform, the gizmo, and the X-rock. The gizmo was securely bolted down to the center platform. X-rock was held in position by cables so that every part of the rock was available for rubbing. The battery was firmly fastened down behind the gizmo.

To ensure secrecy during the procedure, the X-rock was shielded by a blanket. Only Bernie and Ludwig had a full view since they were the ones making the connections. A rainbow of color was visible, but not enough for anyone else on the surgical team to see.

The techies, Ludwig and Charlie, were making all of the electrical connections.

Charlie yelled, "Watch out! Some of the connections are sparking. We don't need short circuits here."

Ludwig screamed, "Nurse, keep the moisture out of my eyes so I can see what I'm doing."

His rudeness indicated to the nurses how stressed he was.

The nurses were constantly wiping the sweat off the techies' foreheads.

Bernie, Charlie, and Ludwig finished putting on the final touches.

"Thank goodness, we have finished," said Ludwig.

Bernie echoed the sentiment, and added, "We have to wait for him to come out of anesthesia."

Wreck resisted waking up because of the pleasant dreams he had while under; he didn't want to leave the fantasies.

As Wreck was coming out of the deep sleep, he called out, "Where am I? I need to get home. What's going on?"

Nurse Abby stroked Wreck's right fender and said, "It's okay. You just had surgery. Settle down. Everything is fine."

It took a half hour for him to get his wits back. Finally, he realized where he was. "Thank you for your concern. I'm okay now."

***

The news spread quickly that the operation had been completed, and everybody gathered again outside

Charlie's boathouse. Harry put Bart the black bear and Kim the darling deer in charge of crowd control.

What a sight! The crowd applauded, cheered, and sang the "Wreck Song":

"Wreck, oh, Wreck.
Oh, what the heck, we love you so,
Stay strong as always, be not afraid.
We are here, beloved friend,
So don't let the air out of your tires,
Keep on rolling, keep on rolling!"

The team rolled out Wreck to face a battery of microphones.

"Thank you, everyone, for your good wishes. The song is over the top. It's wonderful. Thank you again."

After hearing a few other speeches, the crowd slowly dispersed, feeling relieved and happy, and went about their daily routines.

The surgical team members were still dripping black slimy oil due to the infamous ruptured line. They had plenty of time to degrease later.

***

They rolled Wreck back into the boathouse, where he would recoup for a couple of days. The doors were left open. This way, as he was resting he could look out at the pond and watch the residents going about their everyday activities.

The quiet time gave him the opportunity to reflect about many significant things that were now important to him. The one thing he kept thinking about was his trip into dreamland. What wonderful feelings they had been! He knew these feelings would stay with him forever.

***

The evening of the surgery, townsfolk held a candlelight vigil at the boathouse. They hummed and softly sang the "Wreck Song."

They stayed for twenty minutes. When they were leaving, they waved to him and he waved back with his right tire. Wreck's emotions were hard to control; he let his tears flow.

He knew having the surgery had been the right decision.

Chapter 13

Two days after the transplant, Wreck moved back into his garage.

***

Harry, Sally, Charlie, and Ludwig were sitting by the pond with Wreck to debrief his surgery. He said he felt as good as new. In fact, never in his life had he felt better!

Ludwig confided that there had been a few critical moments during the surgery. He asked Wreck, "Do you recall any time that stands out while you were under anesthesia?"

"Yeah, I remember a couple of different things. One was that I was traveling up this gold-colored road and around me were open green fields. Birds were flying around, singing, and all kinds of animals were playing and having fun. They seemed so carefree and happy."

Sally's curiosity was piqued. "How did it make you feel?"

"Peaceful."

"What happened next, Wreck?" asked Harry, his hind legs dangling over the edge of the seat.

"I rolled up to big pearly gates that opened, and I could see inside. I saw all kinds of folks and cars, playing, eating, and having the time of their lives."

Harry chuckled. "Sounds like my kind of place."

"Then I saw my parents with big smiles on their grilles, motioning for me to come in. And before that, I met the car of my dreams."

Sally said, "Oh, please tell us more."

"Ahh, she was so beautiful, with gleaming chrome hubcaps and a wax job so shiny I could see my face in the reflection. Little Wrecks were rolling around and playing, like kids do. I thought, *Wow, a family with the girl of my dreams.*" Recalling the sight, Wreck sighed with pleasure.

"Please continue," said Ludwig in a serious tone. To him, this was all about science.

"I remembered the work I still have to do for Pond-ville. I felt a tug from both sides—each trying to pull me in their direction—and I knew I had to make a decision as to which way to go. I thought about my friends in Pondville, and a powerful feeling came over me. You can't let your friends down," Wreck said, shaking his head. "Who else could fill my shoes—I mean, tires. I knew my dream place wouldn't go away. It would still be here at a later date. That's the moment when I decided to make the commitment to my friends."

"Wreck, how touching," Sally said, "and how happy I am that you are still here."

Wreck resumed. "One thing stands out in my mind. I was looking down at myself and saw Bernie trying to grab an oil line that was flopping around, and the whole surgical team was trying to stop the oil from squirting out."

Ludwig chimed in, "They were probably hallucinations from the anesthesia."

It seemed as if Ludwig was trying to pooh-pooh the dream.

"Maybe, and then, maybe not," Wreck responded with a hint of a grin on his grille.

"Well," Ludwig said, "let's get started with the testing and see how everything works. I think we've heard enough about your dream adventures. They were quite impressive. Are you ready?"

"You bet I am. I can't wait a minute longer."

Harry jumped in behind the steering wheel, Ludwig sat in the passenger seat, and Sally hopped into the back, along with Charlie. They were both squished onto the rumble seat and their feet rested on a step board. They sat higher than the others and could see everything going on around them. Everyone fastened their seat belts. This was the inaugural voyage and the drama was intense.

What if it didn't work?

What would they do?

Would Wreck be okay?

Would the test drive hurt him?

Wreck was excited with anticipation, not knowing what he might feel.

Harry turned the key to start Wreck. The sheriff put the gearshift in forward, stepped on the gas pedal ... and off they went.

Sally's hair blew back as the wind flowed through the open car.

The passengers clapped with relief. The gizmo worked perfectly. What a smooth ride!

Harry tried slowing down by pressing on the brake. "Uh-oh, we have a stopping problem!"

Charlie said, "Not to worry. It needs a slight adjustment."

Traveling up the steepest part of the hill, Wreck had no ill effects and no backfiring.

Harry made several turns using the steering wheel. "Hey, the steering wheel doesn't respond instantly. There's a delay, and that could be a big problem."

Again, Charlie made light of it. "Another adjustment here, another there, and it's a done deal."

Ludwig said to everyone, "Adjustments were to be expected. Overall, I'm really feeling good about the way the gizmo is working."

They headed down to the racetrack to make one lap around the pond.

Afterward, Charlie said, "Let's stop at the boathouse, and I'll make the adjustments."

***

Several days had passed since the test drive. Each day Harry and Sally strolled over to Wreck's garage and took him out for a roll around the pond. The two frogs often sat on a park bench and chatted about life in general.

The highlight of their day was when Wreck would say, "Hop in, you two. Let's take a ride around town."

Rolling along at the speed limit, they could enjoy the fresh air and the scenery.

Sally remarked, "Look, there's Fifi the fox, walking with the cubs. How cute!"

"Judge Isabella, good morning," Harry called out. He slowed down and tipped his hat.

The judge was rushing to the courthouse because she had a trial starting in a few minutes. Ever polite, she stopped to greet them. "Good morning, everyone. Lovely day. You are looking quite spiffy, Wreck."

"Why, thank you, Judge. It would be my pleasure to take you for a ride soon."

"Thank you, Wreck. I would love that. Court is waiting. Bye."

The sights they encountered while driving around Pondville gave them more to talk about.

It was fun watching the residents going about their daily routines and the youngsters playing in and around the pond.

The ride to the top of the hill was fun in itself because Wreck took a path over many bumps and into potholes.

At each one, Wreck commented, "Whoa, whoa" or "Sorry about that." Or "Oops!"

It was like riding a dirt bike. They were laughing and giggling. It took their minds off anything that made them feel bad.

Chapter 14

"Off to the boathouse we go," Harry said to Wreck and Professor Ludwig.

It was early morning, and Harry assumed his cousin Charlie would be there.

Harry wore his cool sunglasses and his usual sheriff's outfit: his badge attached to his vest, long pants, and a cowboy hat. Ludwig sat in the passenger seat—the copilot's seat, to him. Sporting a beret and a three-piece, tweedy suit, he looked like a proper professor. They both sat straight up in their seats, giving off an aura of being large and in charge.

As they arrived at the boathouse, they saw Charlie leaning on a post on his dock—strumming a tune on his banjo. As usual, he was wearing a Hawaiian shirt and his baseball cap. His tattoos gleamed in the sun.

"Hey, Charlie, open the doors so I can drive Wreck in."

Charlie hopped up, put down his banjo, and ran over to open the doors.

They went inside and settled in for a discussion about making Wreck's body appear new again.

Charlie couldn't wait. He blurted out, "Wreck, have I ever got some ways to make you handsome again. You might even be able to get the girl of your dreams with your new looks!"

"Tell me more."

"Hold on, you guys," Harry said, trying to keep them focused. The last thing he wanted was Charlie to cover Wreck with his tattoo artwork.

Ludwig piped in, "What's our goal here? To change Wreck's original looks or restore him to the original?"

"I was thinking—" Charlie started to give his opinion, but they cut him off.

Harry said, "Stop, stop. Wreck, what do you want?"

"I would really like to be myself, my original design. It suits me. It's who I am."

It was easy to see that Wreck was strong again. He was firm in his wishes. They couldn't argue with his decision.

Charlie was disappointed. He had such grand ideas for Wreck's makeover. However, Charlie knew deep down that Wreck was making the right choice.

"So, we should make a list of what's to be done," Charlie said. "I need to be sure Wreck approves. Besides, I'll need the list in case I have to hunt for any spare parts."

Wreck said, "Before we start making lists, one thing I'd like to do is stay topless. Harry, do you see that as a problem?"

Harry paused, and then answered, trying not to hurt his feelings. "A little bit, but I see where you are coming from, Wreck."

Charlie asked, "What if we make a convertible top that would stay down and only be closed when it rains?"

Ludwig's neck elongated with his enthusiasm. "You know, it sounds like a perfect compromise, Charlie."

"The decision is yours, Wreck," Harry said, and crossed his fingers.

"You guys are brilliant. Of course, the answer is yes. It will make me super cool." Wreck pictured himself as a convertible, all shiny and new.

Harry pulled out the whiteboard, and they made the list. They would need:

1. Leather seats (no bumps)
2. Glistening chrome
3. Bright lights
4. Red and black convertible top
5. New stars
6. Fender work

Ludwig said, "Charlie, can his fenders be resurfaced and repainted? That could save us some money for other things we might need."

"I can't tell right now. If not, I'll scout around and see if I can find suitable replacements at the auto recycling yard. When I'm finished, they'll look as good as new. If I can't find any, we'll have to buy new ones. He's worth it."

Harry asked, "What do we do about the top?"

Ludwig said, "Easy. I'll design the mechanism that rolls up and down to control the canvas. Charlie, will you be able to build it?"

"Yeah. I can build it, and I'll install it."

"I'll check with the manager of the general store and see if they can order a canvas," Harry said. "I have some pull with the manager."

After all, Harry had foiled the store robbery and captured the perpetrators. It had been a major event in Pondville the previous year.

They all laughed and agreed with Harry.

Ludwig said, "Charlie, what help will you need to get this done?"

"Well … I'll need help installing the new parts. I'll need three others to help with removing rust, re-chroming, polishing, painting, and … I think that's it. One more thing. Doc Bernie should be involved, to make sure Wreck's health is maintained. This is a big job."

"It certainly is," Ludwig said. "Harry and I will be with you to assist in any way we can."

With a nod, Harry said, "And I know my deputies will want to help, and so will Sally. You'll have a good crew."

They finalized the list and agreed to meet in the morning.

Harry drove Wreck around town on patrol and then put him in his garage. They left the garage door open for the residents who liked to stop by. Their visits always boosted Wreck's spirits.

***

At dawn the next day, Harry drove Wreck to the boathouse. It was full steam ahead. Everybody had his or her assignment for Wreck's makeover. They planned to work through the day, with only a short lunch break.

Because everybody pitched in and there was no time wasted, the job was completed in two days.

Chapter 15

"Wow, look at you, Wreck," Chief Deputy Sheriff Kim said after circling him once. "You look smashing." She had stopped by his garage to visit.

Wreck's grille had the biggest smile ever. "Can I take a look in the mirror?" he asked. "I still haven't seen the new and improved me."

Kim brought over a full-length mirror, and Wreck almost fainted when he saw himself. "I can't believe it. I'm back, and so much better!"

"Yes, you are. You are splendid." Kim was overjoyed for him. "What do you want to do?"

"Go for a ride. I think Harry is coming over soon. The three of us can take a spin around Pondville. Kim, how can I ever repay all of you for your kindness and care?"

"Just continue to be you," said Kim as she polished a fender. "You know how much everyone in Pondville loves you, and now you're cuter than ever." She winked at him.

They didn't have to wait long for Harry.

"Hi, Sheriff," Kim said. "I've been admiring Wreck. He's ready to show Pondville his makeover."

"Good stuff," said Harry. "Let's practice putting his top up and down before we go out. It looks like rain."

A hand crank operated the top. Harry pulled it out of the glove box and showed Kim how to use it. At first, the top wouldn't budge, and Wreck started to worry.

Harry gave him a pat on the hood. "Relax, Wreck. It's a new top. Needs some adjustment and lubrication. We'll head over to Charlie's and get it done."

***

"What a feeling!" Wreck was in his glory while riding over to Charlie's.

It started to drizzle as they got there.

"Hi, cuz," said Harry. "We're having a little trouble getting the top up."

"Let me take a look. Maybe a slight adjustment and a little more lube is all it needs," Charlie said.

He had the top in motion and up in no time.

"Thanks, Charlie. Do you want to go for a spin with us?" asked Harry.

"Love to, but I can't right now. I'm working on my boat engine and it's all apart. Thanks, anyway. Next time?"

Kim glanced outside and said, "Let's keep the top up. It's raining hard out there."

***

The rain didn't bother them a bit. Wreck was savoring every moment of the ride and the approving looks he got. He especially enjoyed the wolf whistles from some of the young pups under cover from the rain.

Wreck was so highly waxed and polished that the rain ran right off him in beads. *If only my dream girl could see me now!*

***

The day after Wreck's makeover, Harry stood in front of the deputies. He toyed with his baton for a moment to collect his thoughts.

"You've seen Wreck and what a remarkable recovery and restoration he has had. What do you think about making him an honorary deputy?"

"It sounds good," said the new deputy, Stinky the skunk, "but he can't arrest anyone or put handcuffs on them. So how could he be a deputy?"

Kim jumped in. "That's why it would be honorary."

Bart picked up from there. "You know, he is definitely a member of the team. He will make our jobs easier, and we'll be able to arrive at trouble spots quicker. Besides, he would make a great witness in court."

"I never considered it that way," said Deputy Earl the crow. "I remember how important my eyewitness testimony was for the general store robbery trial."

"You all make so much sense," Stinky said as he pulled on his farmer jean suspenders. "I didn't see it that way at first. What was I thinking? Of course he should be an honorary deputy. It's a great idea."

"Then we're in agreement. Our discussion will help me with my request to the mayor." Harry planned to meet with the mayor in the morning.

Sheriff Harry wanted to get this done right away in order to show off Wreck. The pride in his new appearance and being appointed an honorary deputy would make Wreck bubble over beyond belief.

***

"Good morning, Mr. Mayor. Do you have time to meet with me now?"

"Sure thing, Harry. Pull up a seat. How're you doing? I hear Wreck has recovered and looks splendid," Mayor Percy said in his usual booming voice.

"I'm fine, Mayor. Wreck is the reason I'm here. My team and I would like to make him an honorary deputy. We already consider him part of our team. Do you approve?" Harry didn't waste any time giving the reasons why. He just wanted a "yes" from Mayor Percy.

"It sounds okay to me, Sheriff. I suppose you'll be swearing him in?"

"Actually, I figured it would be better if you did. It would mean so much to Wreck, and most residents will turn out for a ceremony if you do it."

"Thank you. That's kind of you. I think you're very humble. You'd do just fine, but I appreciate your confidence and I'd be honored. Could you put some words together for me? After all, you know Wreck so well."

"Sure thing. When would you like to have the swearing in?" Harry asked. He didn't want this delayed. Delays had happened before with the mayor.

"Let's do it in two days. I don't think we can schedule it any sooner. That'll give us time to get the word out. I'll ask Sally to post a notice in the Pondville General Store and also to arrange the ceremony."

"Agreed. I'll jot down some notes for you and have Charlie make a deputy sheriff's star for Wreck's hood."

Chapter 16

"You wanted to see me, Mayor?" Sally said, taking a few steps into the mayor's office.

"Yes, Sally. Thank you for stopping in. Let me explain why I asked you here. Have a seat."

Mayor Percy the turtle got comfortable, stretched his arms out, and placed them behind his head. "I know you and Harry are great friends, so you may already know about this. Stop me if you do."

"You know I will, Mayor." She chuckled.

"He asked me to make Wreck an honorary deputy. What do you think of the idea?"

"I love it. I was at the morning meeting when we talked about it. I agree wholeheartedly."

"Wonderful. I will be swearing him in, and I need your help getting everything arranged. You are the perfect one to organize it. I still marvel at the way you run the annual derbies. Do you think you can help me?"

"Absolutely, Mayor. What are you thinking?"

"I want to make it a special occasion for Wreck and for Pondville. We need announcements to get the word out in Pondville. We'll need microphones for the speeches. Perhaps we can have the bear band play a few tunes for the ceremony. There should be a platform at the end of the pond. What do you think?"

"Mayor, it all sounds good. I'll have a few ideas of my own, as you can imagine. I'll run them by you when I'm ready. When do you plan to have the ceremony?"

"Two days from now."

"Two days? It's a stretch, even for me. But you know me. I'll make it happen."

"Thank you, Sally. I knew I could count on you."

***

Sally had called on her usual cohorts: Dana and Greg, the sheep, and Chief Deputy Bart the bear. They worked around the clock to ready everything for the ceremony. When needed, they called on others to help.

The stage was set up.
The mics were tested.
Announcements were posted.
Wreck's deputy badge was made.
The bear band was ready to play.
A plaque was created.

***

Today was the day. Everybody was scurrying around to get things done. Many had worked on events like this before, helping the arrangements go smoother.

All had been accomplished in two days. This was remarkable, even for Sally!

A few minutes before the ceremony, all the key players, except Wreck and Harry, were in place and many residents had arrived. The band was tuning up.

Spotting Wreck and Harry on the track, the band started up with a marching song. Everyone started clapping and a few whistled.

The sheriff and his car pulled up to the stage.

Mayor Percy opened his arms to welcome everyone as he stepped up to the microphone. "Welcome to a very special event for one of Pondville's finest. It is my honor to preside over the swearing in of our newest deputy, Wreck."

The mayor gestured to Wreck, who waited near Harry. "Many of you know that the past year has been difficult for him, and now, look at our restored Wreck. He is magnificent." Percy loved to hear his own voice, and he went on … and on.

"Wreck, please roll up closer. …… Do you swear to honor the duties of an honorary deputy?"

"I do," Wreck said. He raised his right wheel to be sworn in.

"Sheriff, will you please attach his star."

Harry fixed the star onto Wreck's hood and saluted him.

The band started playing again.

Many attendees had tears in their eyes.

The applause went on for a long time.

After it stopped, Mayor Percy asked, "Wreck, would you like to say a few words?"

"Thank you, Mayor," Wreck said. His headlights were blinking on and off—he was deeply touched. "This honor is more than I ever expected. Thank you, Sheriff, and teammates." He winked at his friends in the sheriff's department.

It was amazing what Wreck could do with his headlights!

"My heart is filled to overflowing. Your support means everything to me. I will always be here for my friends and my beloved Pondville."

The crowd couldn't contain themselves. The cheering went on and on. The band started up and played another marching song. Harry got into Wreck and drove down the track to the sound of the lively music.

Refreshments were served in a tent set up near the stage. It gave Mayor Percy a chance to schmooze with residents. Many hung around, talking in small groups. Gradually, everyone left.

Halfway down the track, Harry heard Ludwig yelling, "Sheriff, Sheriff, stop!" Ludwig sounded frantic.

He ran up to the car, and Harry said, "What is it, Ludwig?"

"My lab was robbed!"

***

What did they take?

Who did it?

Why is Ludwig so upset?

Stay tuned for Book 4!

About Dr. Bob's Tales

Dr. Bob's Tales were inspired by my imagining different characters living around a pond. The pond became the centerpiece for the town of Pondville. Pondville turned into a community populated by diverse, relatable, and memorable characters, many of them loveable. The main cast of characters appears in every book. New ones are introduced as the plots unfold in each book. Lessons are taught subliminally. The culture of Pondville is a lesson in itself.

Readers get to know the characters and follow their exploits. For some readers, the Pondville characters become lasting imaginary friendships.

It is through discussing the stories with friends, family, in school, or in book groups that the lessons really pop.

No one can forget the 15th Annual Go-cart Derby in Book 1, *Hurry-Up Harry*, when Harry, Ludwig, Rolf, Stinky, and Charlie speed around the racetrack. It's great to see who has sportsmanship, who doesn't, and who shows up as the winner. Many readers can see themselves through the participants' eyes. Stinky just wants to race and have a good time. Rolf wants to win at all costs, even if he hurts someone else. Who will win?

Book 2, *Harry and the Hooligans*, throws out a challenge to the town and its good citizens. We see Harry maturing and taking over as the sheriff. He forms a wild and wily posse, and they form a plan to catch the hooligans who are robbing the general store. The story is action packed, and shows how "going along to get along" can lead to bad consequences. And, can the hooligans make up for their wrongs?

Book 3, *Harry Saves Wreck*, shows how the leaders in the town and the residents come together to save Wreck, the old sheriff's car. What actions do the Pondville residents take to express how they love and value him?

Book 4 is on the way!

Please enjoy the discussion guide, or create your own.

Dr. Bob

Discussion Guide

1. Harry became the sheriff of Pondville in Book 2 and he matured quite a bit. Now he has to deal with a sheriff's car that is an actual wreck. What changes do you see in Harry as he gets used to Wreck and they become friends?

2. Wreck is not just a car. He is a talking car, and eventually becomes an honorary deputy of the Pondville Sheriff's Department. Talk about his personality. What do you like the most about Wreck? Why? What is one characteristic that you find funny? What is one trait you find surprising?

3. If you could have one friend from this tale, who would it be? Why?

4. Wreck has a wonderful dream when he is under anesthesia during his surgery. Do you ever have wonderful dreams? How do you feel when you wake up, after having one of these dreams?

5. Red is a general, a take-charge ant. He knows his job and talks through a bullhorn. What about him stirred your imagination?

6. Ludwig is an interesting character. How would you describe his attitude? What do you like about him? What about him would frustrate you?

7. Ludwig the turtle and Charlie the frog are a good team. They are different in so many ways. How are they different? What do you think is the secret to their teamwork?

8. Sally is a fun frog and a great organizer. Mayor Percy really relies on her. How does she react when he asks her to take charge of Wreck's swearing in?

9. There are many funny scenes in this tale. Some even make you laugh out loud. Pick out your favorite.

10. There are also some touching scenes in the story. Describe them. What did you feel?

11. What do you think might happen in Pondville after the end of this tale? What story do you think Dr. Bob might tell in Book 4?

12. What is one lesson that you took away from Book 3? How will you apply that lesson?

About the Pond

Foxhill Acres, my former home in Marriotts Cove, Nova Scotia, is a beautiful natural setting and provided me with inspiration. It is home to many of the indigenous creatures upon which my story characters are based. The idea for Harry started when a child heard the frogs croaking in the pond and asked me, "Why?"

ACKNOWLEDGMENTS

With special thanks to the following:

Frances Keiser, my guide, mentor, and designer who started the journey with me. She has always been there with support, encouragement, and information.

Beth Mansbridge, my copy editor who went above and beyond the usual copyediting.

Rose E. Grier Evans, my illustrator who worked tirelessly to create the right illustration each and every time. She collaborated to the nth degree and always with a smile and words of encouragement.

Dr. Ron Jawor, Megan Rainey, and Derek Rainey, my reviewers who gave of their time and provided valuable insights and feedback.

Ann Ernst, my partner in every sense of the word, who encouraged, collaborated, and challenged me as I wrote my third book.

About the Illustrator

Rose E. Grier Evans is an award-winning book illustrator and has been a professional artist for more than thirty years. She was delighted to work with the author again, portraying his vision for *Harry Saves Wreck*, and illustrating his story with whimsical details.

When not working on art projects, Rose is advocating for children or busy tending the goats on the family farm. She lives in North Central Florida with her husband, and enjoys spending time with their two grandchildren and other family members.

ABOUT THE AUTHOR

Dr. Robert A. Ernst is a retired orthodontist who practiced in central Connecticut for more than forty years. His education was interrupted when he joined the Air Force. He became a 1st lieutenant during the Vietnam era, before resuming his educational goals.

His early career as an author began in the form of a storyteller. Known as Dr. Bob, he created tales about the animals that lived around the pond at Foxhill Acres, his home in Nova Scotia, Canada. He delighted neighboring children with the stories. In more recent years, his wife Ann convinced him to write down the stories in a series of books, and Dr. Bob's Pondville was created. More tales are on the way.

Dr. Bob and Ann reside in Florida.

Lightning Source UK Ltd.
Milton Keynes UK
UKHW020339060122
396687UK00002B/55